THE BEGINNING~

I grew up in South Louisiana, Ca little rural town practically dead-ce half of the state, just west of the g. out Atchafalaya Basin. LaSalle was a wonderful place in which to live and to grow up. In the early 1950's there were about 25,000 people living in and around LaSalle. Thinking back it was a simpler time and a time when people seemed to enjoy life more. It certainly wasn't as hectic as life is today. Divorce was a rare occurrence. Mothers stayed at home for child rearing and to provide a pleasant environment for their family. Violent crime wasn't an issue so house doors were seldom locked.

On weekends, holidays, and summer vacations, we had much greater latitude with respect to our personal time and activities. In a time without smart phones it wasn't necessary that we check-in every hour. We would tell our parents where we were going and what we might be doing, and they would tell us when we were expected to be home…usually an hour before supper. In many ways it was as though we lived on a different planet altogether in comparison to today's lifestyle. Most working people went home for lunch which usually was the largest meal of the day. Supper consisted of leftover lunch items.

For a typical lunch Cajun women would prepare fried, stewed, roasted or baked meat (hamburger, chicken, pork, or fish). Items that were included on every table at every meal were: a pot of rice and gravy. Vegetables were plentiful; Beans, Peas, Corn, Okra; real ice-tea; a plate of sliced tomatoes with mayonnaise on the side; a loaf of "Evangeline Maid" bread, with a slab of butter; and desserts, included cakes, cookies, brownies or other sweets, all home-made. Other staples were: chicken & sausage gumbo or seafood gumbo, shrimp or crawfish (in season) Etoufee, smoked sausage, Andouille, Boudin, Jambalaya, Red beans & rice, Stuffed Bell peppers or Cabbage Rolls, and many others dishes.

A typical work week looked like this: Monday, Tuesday, and Wednesday morning until noon; Thursday, Friday, and Saturday morning until noon. And, in the smaller towns that dotted the countryside... around LaSalle on Sundays there were far more horse-drawn carriages tied up in front of the local church than there were automobiles. French was spoken in practically every household, particularly among the elderly, and grandparents. People acted happier and visited others frequently. Greetings included sayings such as these: "Mais, how y'all are?: Y'all get down and come inside; How's yo' mama and dem'? Comment ça va?

Those days, the LaSalle area economy was primarily farming. Big oil had come to town, but it hadn't captured the economy as it did in the ensuing years. Field crops were Sugar Cane, Rice, Cotton, Sweet Potatoes (Yams), Corn, and a mix of Beans (not soy) and Peas. There were a lot of small farms and ranches. For those of you city-slickers who may not know the difference between them, farms grow field-crops; ranches grow livestock, cattle, horses, poultry but mostly beef cattle. Beef cattle in the area were a mix of breeds, Angus, Herefords, Limousins, and Brahma, but most were Cracker cattle or Swamp Cattle as they're called in Louisiana.

Swamp cattle are a breed of cattle that were introduced in the 16th Century by the Spaniards, first in Florida and then along the Gulf coast. These small cattle, by comparison, are a most hardy and durable breed that has flourished in the 500-years since they were introduced to the New World. The following incident occurred in the same time period and is representative of events of the day. Insofar as Swamp cattle are concerned as it is an example of their ability to endure the hostile environs found along our Gulf coast.

Louisiana has always been pestered by mosquitoes. In the years leading up to the 20th century, mosquitoes were responsible for the spread and devastation of Yellow-Fever in which many, many thousands died. However, after the last epidemic ended in 1905, and scientists at last discovered the role that mosquitoes played in the spread of that disease, yellow-fever ceased to be a problem. While the plague may be history its carrier remains to plague Louisianans' to this day The mosquitoes that rise up out of the marshes of our fair state must have been mutated by some devilish fiend operating deep in our swamps for these critters are large...much larger than your average 'skeeter. These bad girls (everyone knows it's just the females that bite you, right?) Well these ladies don't bite...they sting! And, if you should squish one, they'll virtually explode with blood.

On this particular day I am seated in a duck blind in the marshes of Vermilion Parish, Louisiana, approaching that time referred to by duck hunters as the "Magic Moment", that moment when the first glint of light appears on the horizon signaling the opening of the day's hunting. It is at that time of day when your eyes begin scanning the horizon for flights of ducks. I don't see any ducks, but what I do see is a small, impenetrable cloud drifting my way. I recognize it as a swarm of marsh 'skeeters. Now, I'm talking about 'skeeters that make you shrink in fear when you first observe their size and their ferocity. The only thing between me and the oncoming cloud of blood-thirsty insects is a thin veil of netting covering my face.

No part of my flesh is exposed to this threat. Behind my veil I watch intently. This wasn't my first time to suffer such an assault. Nevertheless, no matter how many times one experiences these encounters it is not lacking in drama. The swarm, numbering in the thousands has now enveloped me, completely covering the netting over my face as the 'skeeters frantically attempt to reach my flesh. A barely perceptible sound occurs accompanied by a slight, discernible movement in the netting each time 'skeeters strike it. A person suffering from claustrophobia would no doubt panic under this onslaught.

Fortunately as the sun breaks free from the horizon the swarm dissipates and moves off in search of another less protected victim. No wonder these critters have been known to drive elephants crazy in Africa. But this ain't Africa, Leroy, although it just as soon as be. From this memory I'm teleported to an earlier time-line, a summer day when I accompanied my dad to Cameron, Louisiana, the parish seat for, Cameron Parish.

It was late summer of '57 and the memories and effects of Hurricane Audrey were fresh on everyone's mind and the horrific evidence of that cataclysmic event was everywhere still. I don't know what ground-zero looks like and I hope I never do, but I imagine it looks an awful lot like what I saw that day. Cameron (orig. Leesburg) is, was and always will be nothing more than a fishing village and jumping-off spot for offshore oil. It's hard to believe that anyone would really want to live in Cameron, in fact statistics show otherwise. However, the town stands as a testament to man's will having barely survived at least fourteen (14) hurricanes, three (3) catastrophic hurricanes beginning with the unforgettable Hurricane Audrey in 1957, which claimed over 500 lives, followed by Hurricane Rita in 2005, and Hurricane Ike in 2008. Little wonder the town's population is down 80% since 2000.

The town itself is situated near the heel of the Louisiana coastline just south of Calcasieu Lake. The landscape was littered with wreckage. Mobile homes, which were in abundance, were all destroyed as was every other commercial or residential structure. Trees sheared in half or uprooted lay everywhere along with broken telephone poles. Twisted metal from buildings and signage were scattered far and wide including pieces or parts of machinery, cars, and boats, small and large dotted the landscape. The most dominant structure in the town, for that matter the only structure was the weather-beaten courthouse which was to Cameron what the Super Bowl was to New Orleans in providing a place of refuge for displaced citizenry during ruinous hurricane disasters.

The reason the carnage was so severe in the case of Audrey, was that those days were before the weather alerts we now have. The residents of Cameron were caught completely unaware of the impending doom that was to befall them. As a hurricane, Audrey was not all that severe, but its tidal surge, a wall of water 12-feet high was devastating. The residents were still recovering from its effects. Fishing boats and tug-boats of enormous size were found twenty miles from the coast. Practically every structure in Audrey's path was washed away, save the courthouse building.

My dad was buying Oil & Gas leases for Texaco at that time and he had scheduled meetings with some mineral owners that afternoon. People were desperate for money so my dad was welcomed with open arms by the Cajun owners. Before his meetings we went to the courthouse and I had the privilege of "pulling books" for him. Here's a back breaking exercise if ever there was one. Now for those of you who don't know, back in those days the record books and their indices (plural for index, although now they're simply referred to as indexes) of the Clerk of Court's Records were books made for the Nephilim (look it up, but basically, "Giants"). I don't know whose idea it was to create 40-pound books the size of the hood on a Buick "Roadmaster"? There had to be reasoning behind that idea, but what? I still can't figure that one out?

In those days the clerks had to transcribe each recorded document into these books, while the original documents were stored in a vault. Thankfully, with the advent of copiers and later computers these books were downsized to a much more manageable size and for all intents and purposes eliminating the "heavy lifting" of those days. The indexes were laid out on slant-topped (?) counters and were organized by year and last name...Vendor/Vendee. My dad ran the indexes and would then hand me a piece of paper with the books containing the instrument he needed to peruse. I swear he managed to find a way so that each book I had to retrieve was either on the very bottom shelf or the very top shelf. After hoisting, delivering and replacing some twenty or so books I was ready to take a break.

We finally did break for lunch and ended up at I believe the only restaurant in town at that time. After lunch we ventured out into the hinterlands along Highway 27 (Creole Nature Trail) towards Creole, Louisiana, a place where "wide spot in the road" is being generous. After meeting with his mineral owners and getting some leases signed we began our return trip to LaSalle. It was late afternoon by then and the sun hung low in the summer sky. On the north side of the highway where many Swamp cattle grazed there were huge "smokes" built by the ranchers to protect their cattle against the daily swarms of mosquitoes. These smokes (fires intended to produce an abundance of thick, heavy smoke) were built using old trees, tires, crop residues, Neem leaves (another lookup) and other such material, and coal oil was the accelerant of choice. Cattle would stand in long lines that led up to the smokes. Several cows could be seen standing in this smoke. One group would stand in it for a couple of minutes before moving off, allowing for the next group of cows to enter the smoke. It was an amazing site to see as these creatures seemed to understand that the smoke would protect them from the mosquitoes and each instinctively knew it only had a limited time to stand in the smoke before relinquishing their place for the next cow waiting patiently in line. This was my first encounter with this practice that has been used for centuries around the world. It's not really understood what the smoke does to lessen the assault of mosquitoes, but it does seem to have a repelling effect. I think the smoke tends to mask the scent of warm bloodied mammals which makes it harder for mosquitoes to "see" us. I could be wrong?

About halfway between Creole and nowhere, which is about 10-miles in any direction from BFE, the car swerved suddenly followed by that sickening sound of thump-thump-thump-thump, the sound of a tire going flat. Dad didn't bother to pull off on the shoulder because there wasn't any shoulder. Even if he had we would have really been in a fix in that soft "gumbo" loamy soil. My dad was not one to use profanity reserving such outbursts for special occasions…this was one of those occasions. There we sat staring out the windshield ahead where swarms of mosquitoes were billowing up out of the marshes.

He looked at me and said, "We'll take turns on changing this tire. I'll go first then you'll have to spell me. OK? You understand?" I nodded grimly knowing all too well that we were fixing to get out asses chewed-up by several-billion 'skeeters. I wished we could have stood in the smoke at that moment. Dad got out, managed to open the trunk and unscrew the foot of the jack which secured the spare in place, and was able to set the jack before succumbing to the onslaught of the mosquitoes. He looked like he was a madman dancing the jitterbug as he swatted the cloud of unrelenting bugs covering him. Finally, he was back in the car bringing a small swarm with him. "Alright, son, you're up." I took a deep breath and jumped into the fray.

I had no idea what I was getting into. The mosquitoes were everywhere…in my eyes, in my nose, my ears, my mouth…it was, to say the least, horrific. I managed only to get the car partially jacked up before I had to surrender. Dad was back out and he managed to remove the flat tire, I was back out securing the tire with the lug-wrench which was a slow, tiresome exercise, but by now I had become a madman as well cursing and swatting the air wildly as I struggled to tighten the last lug nut in place. Dad finished up for us, throwing the flat tire into the trunk along with the tools.

By the time we arrived back home we had scratched ourselves raw. That night I slept without bed covers as my entire body was alive with itchiness. Much later, I finally drifted off to sleep, the smell of calamine lotion hanging heavy in the air.

Now back to the types of cattle found in Louisiana in those days, ca.1950 ...and there were Dairy cows which were primarily Holstein. At least that's what I remember mostly was Holsteins, I know there were others. On the horse side, it was Quarter Horses for riding, roping, and racing... and very few if any Thoroughbreds. In between those categories, there was a little bit of everything else, from vegetable farming to hog farming. The countryside around LaSalle obviously reflected the farming industry, mostly pastures and fields, but there were also vast wooded areas as well particularly along Coulees (small creek or stream, from the French word, "to flow") and along the bayous and rivers as well as other places.

In the old days land was always attached or bounded on one side or other but water, the staff of life, for crops and cattle but equally important for travel, for there were no roads in those days.

Everything moved on water. And the timber that grew in large stands along the banks of these waterways and in the water was vitally important for construction of houses, barns, fence posts, furniture and the like, and for burning in fireplaces or stoves. Bald Cypress, Tupelo Gum, Oaks are predominate in the swamps or wetlands. Further inland, Live Oaks, Southern Pine, Water Oaks, Pecan, Hackberry, Gum, and on and on. The list is extensive.

The early land grant tracts on the Mississippi River ran from the river back towards the wetlands or swamp. These were also found along the navigable streams of southern Louisiana, and as we as along major waterways in other areas. These were known as French arpent land divisions (Arpent: a measure of land equal to 0.85 acres of land). These are long narrow parcels of land four-sided, but pie-shaped, ranging from 2 to 8 arpents on the frontage (river side) and usually 40-arpents deep. This method of land division provided each land-owner with river frontage as well as land suitable for cultivation and habitation. Typically, the rear boundary was covered with bottomland woods or swamp, but needless to say, with a heavy growth of timber.

In the 1950's, people hunted lands freely, although it was cordial to stop in to see the landowner and to make certain he was okay with your being on his property. Usually speaking if the land wasn't posted it was OK to hunt on it. Often times the land owner was harvesting his own crop for his and his family's needs. This could mean Alligators or maybe doves or ducks, but in any event those certain species that were forbidden and you couldn't take any of them without incurring the landowner's wrath. If you hunted an owner's property, you took care to be respectful in your conduct, noting where livestock was located and closing and latching any gates you may have opened. Species such as squirrels or rabbits were okay to hunt almost anywhere. If you had a good days hunt you might leave a couple of ducks, or some doves or squirrels for the owner.

It is illegal to take any Robins, but in our younger years we shot many a Robin and Blackbirds as well. Robins are excellent eating birds and we had many a meal off our takes…we'd breast'em out like doves and cook them over an open fire. Good eating! So, it was in this environment that we tramped through and over untold hundreds of miles of farmland and woods, seeking adventure wherever we went.

There was a camp belonging to the Popler family that was located southwest of LaSalle on Saloon Road that was a favorite place from which we conducted a great many of our forays into the countryside. Brent Popler and his older brother Cary were both good friends of mine and I was a regular visitor to their camp for many years. Across Saloon Road were lands belonging to the Burgan family that extended from the opposite side of Saloon Road facing Popler's Camp to the Little Red River, a distance of about a quarter mile, more or less. A gravel road permitted access from Saloon Road to the river where the Burgans had a large camp. The road was covered by a thick canopy of trees and ground cover on either side so dense as to obscure the road altogether. We explored this property regularly often-times stopping at an isolated, old pond about 50 to 60-paces west of the gravel road. This pond was so secluded that it would go unnoticed walking past it if one weren't aware of its presence. It was about a three acre pond, no more than waist deep and home to a large frog population.

We frequently made stops there to look for the possibility of any snakes slinking about. Wherever you find an abundance of frogs, you'll also find snakes and Snake hunting, for a time, was one of the main reasons for our venturing into the woods. We hunted snakes with a passion, the Popler brothers, and Mike Montague and me. Occasionally Rex Verot joined us. All of us at one time or another had king snakes as pets, usually the speckled or salt and pepper variety. But we didn't limit our snake exploits to capturing non-venomous snakes; we also hunted and killed many water-moccasins or cottonmouths (so named for their white mouths) and also copperheads which were not as plentiful as cottonmouths.

After dispatching the snake's head we'd skin'em out and keeping their hides as trophies to display or for use on belts or hat bands. We'd stretch the skins out on wooden planks attaching them with upholstery tacks. Once stretched we'd scrape the skin gently removing any excess meat or fat. A thin layer of salt was then evenly applied before placing the skins in the sun for curing which usually took about a week. Once the skin had dried thoroughly we'd remove all of the salt with warm water. Next, we'd gently rub a mixture of alcohol and glycerin to both sides of the skins to insure they would be supple. Then, we'd hang them in a closet on a piece of clothesline using clothespins until completely cured. The skin would then be rolled and placed in a cool, dry place for storage for a couple of weeks.

And, that's how we did it back in the '50's. At the height of my snake killing days I had a large cardboard box full of skins, squirrel tails and crow's feet. The crow's feet were stretched so that the toes were splayed and the lower leg was upright. After a few days the foot would be attached to a piece of wood and the wood would then be glued to a piece of rock, making an interesting paperweight. I wish I still had that box today.

In any event, once we were on a snake we would pursue it until we had it cornered or until it finally turned on us in a threatening maneuver. We always carried hiking poles or snake poles made from a stout tree limb whose base was sufficiently wide enough to trap a snake's body under it. Once we had the snake's neck beneath the base of our pole we would then grab it as close to its head as possible. Thinking back we were pretty daring in our handling of these poisonous snakes, but we were always very careful to make sure we had a tight grip behind the head clamping the neck between our index finger and thumb and holding the body extended in our free hand to keep it from coiling around the "hot" hand, the one holding the snake's head. If we were going to release the snake, which was unusual, nonetheless caution had to be taken as a release could be as hazardous as a capture. The best method to insure that the snake wouldn't strike you during release was to separate yourself from the snake as quickly as possible which meant standing sideways and flinging the snake head first across your chest.

As an aside: All our snake handling skills were self-taught in the field. We learned just by doing them; scary huh? Do you think our parents ever inquired about our handling of these snakes? Uh-uh! My mama used to tell her friends how she'd go out and replenish the salt on the skins laying out on the top of the pump-house (in those days we lived in an area where we had well water and each well had a pump unit which was housed in a small shed, the size of a large dog-house. I laid my skins out on the top of the pump-house for drying.) But our snake hunting days came to an abrupt end one summer day when Brent was bitten on the hand by a water-moccasin and big brother, Cary, rushed him to the hospital. I visited Brent the next day in the hospital and was stunned to find that his had swollen to the size of a catcher's mitt. Who would have known a hand could swell to such proportions? Brent recovered fully, but that incident ended for good our zest for snake killing.

However, long before that fateful day, we were all spending a weekend at the Popler camp. it was the summer of '58, as I recall. Cary, Brent, Mike, Rex and I were reminiscing about our day. We had filled it doing the usual things we did when out there which meant hiking, killing snakes and, on this occasion, floating a mile or so down the Little Red River so we could jump-off the Broussard Road Bridge. We had a couple of life-jackets we tied together and we entered the river upstream near Burgan's camp, floating en mass downstream on the current to the bridge. At one point Brent gave chase to a fat water moccasin swimming about 10-feet in front of us, Brent got close enough to take a swipe at it with his machete, but he missed. Cottonmouths swim with their whole body on top of the water so they're real easy to spot. The snake ducked under water when Brent missed him and that freaked him and the rest of us out so we quickly abandoned the chase.

In those days the river still had barge traffic and the bridges crossing it had to compensate for the tugboats that pushed strings of barges laden with shell, rock or other composite materials up and downstream. The bridges along the river were vertical-lift bridges, bridges that lifted a section of span by way of a system of cables and counterweights which were strung from 4-lift piers, one at each corner of the span. I mention this because we were jumping from the railing of the bridge itself and some places higher up than that. We made our ascent on the bridge by climbing the protection piers jutting out into the water on either side of the bridge. These bulwarks, made of huge telephone-like poles only larger, not only protected the infrastructure of the bridge itself, but funneled the barges by guiding them into the mouth of the channel (Side Note: At this time the channel was roughly 10-feet deep and 100-feet wide) .

A couple of days later my mama casually mentioned in an off-handed sort of way, "Oh, did you boys enjoy jumping off the Broussard Road Bridge the other day?" Now my mama had a nose for everything we did especially that which we shouldn't have been doing. If we had been smoking or drinking she knew the instant we crossed the threshold of the backdoor. It wasn't until years later that we understood that cigarette smoke permeated clothing. She had a spy network in place that would have been the envy of J Edgar Hoover. As to our bridge incident, she later confessed that a friend had observed our escapade. It was then I remembered that a party barge floated past us as we were frolicking atop the bridge, but since I didn't recognize anyone on board we simply waved as they passed underneath us. This only reinforced the notion that you can never be absolutely certain that your actions would not fall under the gaze of unexpected witnesses. Add to that, my being a redhead naturally made me a stand-out from the rest of the crowd and I was well known by my parent's circle of friends.

Anyway, putting that aside, after a half hour or so of jumping off the bridge into the murky depths of the Little Red River, so called because of its red tint, we climbed the protection piers of the bridge for the last time and crossed over to the south-side of the river. We made a stop at the old country store just down the road from the bridge for cold drinks and a snack, before continuing on our hike back to the Popler camp. The old country store (whose name is lost to history) was ancient in those days. Old gravity-fed gas pumps long retired stood like silent sentinels out in front. Made almost completely of old "Pecky" Cypress boards. The old store creaked and groaned with every step you'd take. Inside you could find damn near everything from donuts to dynamite. In the back of the store were two double-wide doors opening onto a loading dock where grain, feed and supplies went in and out. In the summer, the doors were kept open all day to permit a behemoth box fan which provided the best circulation of air to be found anywhere in the area. This enormous fan was capable of sucking insects, small birds, and a whole lotta air from outside. The air filtered through every crack and crevice in the store and exited right out the back, cooling the air as it went. We sat on the floor of the loading dock our legs hanging off the edge and took advantage of the coolest breeze around.

After 20-minutes or so of sitting on the loading dock our butts were pretty well stove up and we were dreading the walk back to camp. After being on the go in the heat all-day, swimming down river a couple miles and climbing and jumping off the Broussard Bridge, we were dog-ass tired; and we were still facing a hike home in the hot summer sun. From the store to the Popler camp was roughly a mile and a-half (mol). However, if we cut-off the corner at the Babineaux/Saloon Road intersect we could shorten our walk by roughly a quarter mile give or take. The only problem with this route was we had to cross the Babineaux Brahma Ranch lands. We decided it was worth it. Trudging home across the open field we could see several Brahmas in the distance gathered under the shade of a stand of life-oak trees and it looked as though they hadn't even noticed us.

Now, young men are driven by all sorts of impulses, some good, some not so good, and some just plain crazy and Mr. Crazy was about to show-up. Mike, at least I remember it being Mike, but it could well have been anyone of us. No matter, the thought occurred that it would be great fun to call-out the bulls. We had done this on several occasions and it was a great adrenaline rush to out run a Brahma bull. Of course we usually did it when we were in relatively close proximity to a fence line and in no real danger of being trampled. But this time we were 100 yards from a fence when Mike cut loose with his finest bull call. I must admit we were all very good at imitating a bull, perhaps a little too good. At first there was no discernable movement in the herd and they were still a long way off. However, with Mike's prompting our joining in with his calling, one Mr. Pissed-off bull appeared in the distance and looked to be closing the gap between him and us. Realizing 2,000-pounds of beef on the hoof was bearing down on us we mustered our strength to reach the fence line before the bull reached us. It was an amazing feat…proving once again that the human body can achieve unattainable goals with the proper inducement and incentive.

After several minutes of gasping for breath we were refreshed to the point where we could laugh about it…even brag about it. The truth of the matter be known? The bull wasn't even that close, but that didn't sit well for a good storytelling. We were always told that a Black Angus bull will go through a fence while a Brahma bull will jump it. I've seen many a Brahma bull climb the gates in rodeos so we were glad he was on his side of the fence and we were on ours.

Back at the Poplar camp at last we lounged, relaxing our wearied bodies while discussing the day's adventures and, after eating an evening meal, we decided to go out to the Bergan pond across the road and scare up a mess of bullfrogs. It was still early in the evening when we struck off. A faint whiff of honeysuckle wafted in the evening air on a light, Summer-night's breeze as Mother Earth cast off her mantle of heat from another hot, humid day. It was a relatively cool, moonless night and the natural canopy of tree limbs and foliage hanging over Burgan Road that sheltered us from the sun during the day, created the odd feeling of a descent into a cavernous tunnel. The beams from our flashlights only heightened that effect. The woods on either side of the road were alive with sound, the incessant whirring and humming of insect life, the searing rasp of night calls from the male cicadas, accompanied by the crunching of gravel under our boots. Creepy shadows created by the beams from our lights danced about us, reinforcing the eerie effect of a foreboding tunnel. We spoke little during our trek to the pond.

As we reached the take-off point to go to the pond, I was seriously considering calling it a day and going back to the camp, but I knew I'd never hear the end of that. By comparison the walk to the pond was a short trek, thank goodness, 'cause it crossed some of the thickest woods you'd ever want to walk in. Difficult as it was to cross during the day, crossing at night was a test of endurance. We hadn't gone but a few steps before we were embraced by the thick bramble of choking woods. Climbing vines reached out to entangle us in their snares, stickers and prickly vegetation snagged us, tagged us, and jabbed us. Low hanging limbs of sapling trees slapped at us and the brush of spider webs clung to our skin, amplifying the intensity of the woods as it slowly closed in around us. I felt a pressing urge to run, but I resisted for the fear of falling was very real and meant being engulfed in the unseen writhing clutches of this wooded labyrinth. In spite of that, my steps were quickened, motivated primarily by the thought of the spiders that were lurking and crawling around in the dark. These weren't your typical little wood spiders, these were Golden Orb-Weavers aka, Banana Spiders, a formidable looking spider whose very presence strikes fear in people such as me.

These arachnids are found in great abundance in the woods of South Louisiana. Now, snakes, even the poisonous ones, I could handle, literally, but spiders? Whoa Nellie! That was another thing all together. I have always been deathly afraid of spiders since my early childhood, and spiders the size of a small animal? Fugetaboutit! I found myself thinking over and over. "Banana Spiders don't really grow that big... No! They really don't... Bull-Shit! Yes they DO!" I couldn't get my mind past the fact that as I trudged through this jungle that big spiders weren't beginning to crawl all over me. I have this recurring nightmare...which goes something like this. I'm walking down a gravel road with dense, dark woods on either side, much like the road we just walked. Music from The Twilight Zone can be heard in the background and Rod Serling is clearing his throat. A couple hours have now passed and you're walking back up that very same road. It is almost dark. Actually its dusk...meaning there's no more of that 30-minutes of light left in the day... outside, maybe, in one of the many surrounding fields, but inside on the gravel road with its natural cover and barrier of limbs and foliage, it's already dark-thirty.

Switching on a trusty flashlight a fleeting thought enters your mind, "Did you remember to replace the old batteries in your flashlight the other day, Zippy?" Up ahead the beam of your light shines on several colored objects. Drawing nearer you realize that the colored objects are in fact very large and very real spiders suspended in mid-air, about 3 to 5-feet off the ground. Panic sets in and you desperately scan the darkness with your flashlight seeking an alternate route that will steer you way clear of "Spiderville". You frantically probe the tomb-like darkness with your shaky and diminishing beam of light as you discover to your horror that the roadway is a teeming mass of enormous spiders all hungry and all waiting to sink their fangs deep into the flesh of an intruder unlucky enough to trip its web. Where did all these spiders come from, anyway? How the Hell did they build these webs so quickly, anyhow...and who's the Hell's in charge of this dream!? It's at that moment you realize you are totally alone, and as you recoil in abject terror you grasp a glimpse of the horrible death that awaits you.

For those of you unfamiliar with Banana Spiders let me enlighten you. They can and do build large webs in record time and they are found in great abundance as described above and they are as scary looking as the Alien Queen and her brood of spider-like face-huggers. But enough spider talk. Suffice it to say, I survived the spider gauntlet that night and after several very unnerving moments we at last break out of the bramble of woods and into the clearing where the pond is situated.

I ask Rex to use his flashlight to check for any spiders that may be on me. Rex says, "Oh! Holy shit! Do not move, man. Trust me...do not move!" The blood drains from my brain and I feel faint. "Get it off! Get it off! I scream. Rex breaks out in uncontrollable laughter. Thankfully there were none and my heart now slows from 300-bpm to a normal rate. Above us a star studded sky embraces us, covering us with a dazzling cathedral of heavenly light and reassuring us that God is in Heaven and that He had seen fit to deliver us from the snares of the dreaded woods. Gazing into the eternal depths of the universe, we stood motionless for a moment in awe of the splendor above us. Slowly our senses adjust to our terrestrial surroundings as the chorus of flora Amphibia, a cornucopia of sound swelling in a crescendo of night noise as the songs of a million peepers and tree frogs flood the air, punctuated by the intermittent croaking of bullfrogs lying in the shallows near the water's edge.

Standing upon the worn ring levee that skirts the pond the air is heavy and wet and a fine mist hovers just above the water's black surface. I was the first to step into the pond's murkiness. As it turns out I was the only one. Why am I always the first to do this kinda stuff?. What? Nobody else can do this shit? My rubber boots sink deep into the soft ooze that covered the bottom. I shined my light over its misty surface searching for large yellow eyes that should have been staring back at me along the banks and in the shallows, but there was only the impenetrable mist. Disgusted by the results I turn around to see that the rest of the team is still standing on the ring levee behind me.

At the end of the line is Cary Poplar, oblivious to everything...well, certainly oblivious to me, that's for sure.. He's too busy scanning the pond and all that part of the Parish. He's brought along his trusty 50-Billion-candle power lamp with which he is now sweeping the black night. It looked more like something you'd find mounted on a tower at "Stalag 17". If Sputnik happened to be over-head at that moment, you could rest assure the Kremlin was being notified of a strange light emanating from BFE, Louisiana. Surely Cary sees me? He must see me; I'm standing practically in front of him! Holy Mother of Blessed Searchlights! He doesn't see me! And, at that precise moment the shaft of intense, white light from his lamp burns into my retinas instantly blinding me as if a thousand make that a million, flashbulbs have gone off before me. My pupils have been reduced to pin-pricks. All the while nobody has taken notice of my predicament I knew I should have gone back to camp. I could be raiding everyone's knapsacks right now while these fools are out searching for a frog.

I am standing motionless in the water praying for the restoration of my eyesight when all of a sudden BAM! There wasn't really a Bam, that's just for emphasis. The second my sight is restored a flash of incredible light floods the landscape and everything in our immediate vicinity has suddenly been transformed from pitched-black darkness to brilliantly colored light, as if God had flicked on some heavenly light-switch and the sun miraculously and suddenly appeared in the sky. At that very instant five young boys are mouthing in unison…"WTF!?" The transition for me is slightly more intense as I assess my situation thusly, "Oh, great. My eyesight is restored at the very moment the Ruskies have dropped a 3 megatonne bomb on us. Wait a minute! This is BFE, Louisiana. Not even the Ruskies are that stupid!"

The colors of the pond and the lush vegetation encircling it were dazzlingly vibrant in an array of hues, in such intensity as to make Monet blush…only brighter, much brighter, searingly bright!! (Yeah, I know. "Searingly" It's a made-up word. I do that occasionally when no real word exists that fits the exact feeling or intensity of a situation) In any event, I'd never witnessed such color before or since. We must have looked like a family of Meerkats standing there wide-eyed, mouths agape in disbelief and wonderment. Then a bright glow of light flickered for an instant then dimmed, appearing only as the glow of a half-light of sorts typical of the light one sees when viewing a partial eclipse (those who have witnessed an eclipse, partial or otherwise, know of what I speak), then slowly receding rather than intensifying. It was at that moment we saw and heard, I do not recall in what order it was so sudden, but nonetheless, a giant ball of fire filled the sky. We watched in astonishment as this galactic display unfolded before us. The distinct sounds of flames crackling, licking the cool night air, as a blazing trail of fire is streaming behind.

I do not know if I imagined it or sensed it, but my memory recalls a sensation, a feeling of heat from the broiling object upon my face as it passed over us in the night sky. So close in fact was it that hissing sounds could also be heard. Angry popping noises as gasses were suddenly bursting free from the molten interior in defiance. The object continued across the sky a twisting, writhing ball of flame filled with fury and agony, as if sensing its end was drawing near... it hurled madly against the black sky and then... then... "WTH?"....And then, it disappeared behind the tree line. I wanted to call out, "Wait! Stop! Don't go!" But that would've have been unbelievably stupid! Yet, there was so much more I wanted to see and to know. However, the flaming object's course could not be altered or swayed. It had crossed the untold miles of the universe on its way to a final destination and inevitable destruction and nothing could modify or alter its course.

Immediately a shroud of darkness fell over us once again and we stood there momentarily suspended in a soundless vacuum (is there another sort of vacuum?) Suffice it to say it was quiet, like that moment just before a Sasquatch shows up. Our minds raced to process, sort, and file all the sounds and images we had just witnessed. All at once we were blabbing in unison, exclaiming our perceptions concerning the mysterious object. What was it? Was it the End of the World? Was it a Martian Attack? (The movie, "War of the Worlds", based on the book of the same name by H. G. Wells, had been released a couple of years earlier. In the movie the Martian invasion was engineered by the use of giant fireballs which carried the Martians and their vehicles to earth.)

All at once our clamor was stifled by the sound of a muffled yet thundering, B-O-O-M!" that shook the ground under our feet, signaling the fireball's end as it's reached its final destination many miles in the distance. The sound seemed to roll over us as a wave crashing onto shore and then a hush fell over the pond once again. For a few minutes we scanned the sky, searching for signs we knew not; perhaps evidence of another fireball? But there was nothing save the stillness of the night and the ever-present cathedral of heavenly lights unchanged and once again reassuring us that all was well… that in spite of the brief interlude of frantic turmoil generated by the extraterrestrial intruder, when measured against the backdrop and scale of the vastness of the firmament, it was, in actuality, a flyspeck in time.

We surmised that the object must have gone down somewhere deep in the marshes to the west and south of us in either Vermilion or Cameron Parishes. During this time, Cary had turned off his monster spotlight; however, the rest of us still had our flashlights turned on. Each of us began to sweep our immediate area as we prepared to return to camp. Cary was still standing atop the ring levee when a loud grunt could be heard. It sounded as though it was coming from the opposite side of the pond. The grunt was sufficient to get everyone's attention and freezing us in our tracks. This sound was not typical of the sounds we generally heard in the woods. "What was that?" I offered inquisitively. At the very moment when we were beginning to think it was an imaginary occurrence there was yet another grunt, this one louder than the first. Cary switched on his big-boy light and scanned the opposite bank of the pond. All we could see was the impenetrable mist that floated above the water. Cary swept the far bank again and this time his light detected some slight movement in the mist. Another grunt louder than the previous two served to rivet us in our tracks. Cary was "spot on" literally as a shadowy figure began to materialize out of the mist. I could not believe my eyes. A creature the size of a small building was ascending the opposite ring levee. It was gargantuan in size and there was this terrible odor, as if...well, let's just leave it as terrible. When the thing reached the top of the ring levee it stopped. I could see it was covered in long grey hair, all over its body except for the face. It had black eyes and a cone shape head, and all I could think of was King Kong's baby brother. Through all this, none of us dared move. Cary put his hi-beam directly on the creature's face...which seemed to instantly piss it off. It opened its mouth and let out a roar that I swear resonated so deep in my chest as to make it feel as though the sound was emanating from inside me. I had never felt such a feeling ever before. When he opened his mouth he had a mouth full of square teeth, like a horse. He made a move, a step as if preparing to step down off the levee in our direction. Somebody, everybody I'm uncertain...shouted in unison "RUN!" I swear this sounds crazy, but I remember thinking of Mantan Moreland, the comic, black actor of the 1940's who used to proclaim every time he faced danger, "Feets! Do yo' duty!" Then he'd run like the wind in the opposite direction. A real comic moment...which this definitely was not!

I ran headlong into the terrible woods that, just moments ago, I had lamented having to transverse. The creature was now in pursuit and running in my rubber boots only made me clumsy and ineffectual as a runner. It was every man for himself and I watched Cary breeze by me as if he were running on air, his big-boy light abandoned. I could hear the monster grunting with each step he took as he seemed to draw closer to us. With each footfall he grunted Hunh, hunh, hunh, hunh... and on he came. I was bruised, scratched and bleeding and running out of air as well as my boots. When you're that terrified the body consumes a lot of air needed for the energy you expel.

I tripped over some roots and went down hard, slamming onto my belly and then sliding down a gentle slope into a ditch. I had no sooner come to a rest when I felt the crushing blow from a rubber heel in the middle of my back. One of my team members, no doubt running for his life, had stepped on me causing what air my lungs held to be forcibly expelled. I gasped at the impact. I could hear the creature running behind me, more like thrashing behind me ripping and tearing the flora as he came. I knew I could not get up and run again as he would've been upon me in the matter of a couple of steps. I tried my best to become one with the woods, hoping he hadn't seen me go down.

I became conscious of my breathing and sensed it would give me away if I didn't get control of it. I thought my lungs might explode, but I couldn't permit my body to breathe as much as it needed to. I held my breath pushing my face into the soft damp soil in an effort to disguise or hide my breathing. The creature had stopped running as well I could hear his breathing, he was very close now. Then he made some guttural sounds, as if speaking to…? Oh, my god! Was there another creature? I was so terrified that I couldn't even cry at that moment, but I pissed my pants. I prayed. Oh! How I prayed that

God would let me survive this ordeal. I could hear voices crying out in the distance. They seemed to be a long way off.

The creature hadn't moved a muscle. What was he waiting for? He must not have seen me or he would've certainly been on me by now. It was then that I heard the footfalls of another being heading my way. Heaven help me; there were two of these things. The first one had been waiting for re-enforcements. The second beast barked at the first one as if scolding him. The first beast let out a low moan almost a whimper.

As beast two arrived on the scene I was confronted by the most awful odor one could imagine; a smell of rotting carcasses and waste matter…it was enough to make a buzzard gag. I fought an overwhelming urge to vomit. My stomach was churning and my salivary glands clinched my jaw, a brief signal as my mouth was suddenly filled with slaver. I swallowed, and swallowed again, I would not permit myself the luxury of puking, for it would have most assuredly meant certain death.

The creatures were quiet now except for their heavy breathing. As they stood there, I sensed that they sensed my presence somehow and were waiting for me to reveal my location. Each grunted several times as if frustrated. Oh Lord, I thought, they're practically on top of me. There was some shuffling of feet as if they might be turning to look around, to scan their field of vision. Then I heard them sniffing, sniffing the air. Oh my God, they can smell me, I thought, I'm doomed! But, after a minute or so of sniffing and not being discovered I came to the conclusion that since I hadn't yet bathed that day and that I had, in the course of the day's activities, adorned my body with various sorts of outdoor fragrances such as sweat, river water, mud, snake and bovine funk, and no-telling what-all else? That these odors had masked my presence... blotted-out my human smell.

One creature took a step and I felt the ground beneath me tremble. I prayed he wouldn't step on me because that would've been my death as well. I figured he must have weighed a thousand pounds, maybe more. Then there was another step and another trembling of earth beneath me that was followed by a loud, angry growl that once again resonated deep in my chest. It sounded as though they commenced ripping up trees and vegetation and thrashing about... Oh great!... Now they're really pissed! I heard wood cracking and a shuffling sound. Still I didn't move. I don't know how I managed to hold my breath that long, but I did.

Suddenly another angry roar as if frustration was really setting in. Low, guttural sounds were exchanged between two as if they might be discussing what to do next. Then another incredible roar which was definitely the sound of frustration and I imagined it saying, "I'll get you next time you little bastard!" And, I'm thinking, Yeah, Right! No chance of that happening you big, stinky-ass, ugly Mo-Fo. Unless, of course, you start making house-calls, 'cause if I survive this encounter you won't see my happy-ass in the woods again ...*ever*!".

Then there was the sound of another creature in the distance behind us, but much farther away. It seemed to be calling out. Oh shit! Is there a convention of these ugly bastards going on and we just happened to bust in on it? My guys gave out a couple of whoops and then I heard and felt them walking away, smashing their way through the flora, 'Thump, thump, thump!" I lay there not moving or breathing for the longest time.

When I was certain they had moved off, I rose up on my elbows and took a life-saving breath of air. I lay there for a minute or two relaxing and enjoying the new-found relief of breathing once again. Several minutes passed as I oxygenated my weary body. Then, pulling my arms back on either side of me I placed the palms of my hands on the ground and with what strength remained, I pushed my upper body as if attempting a push-up, but only to point where I could peek over the ditch line. I didn't see or hear a thing. I stayed in that position to be certain they were not around, then I ever so slowly rose into a crouched position, listening for a moment before straightening myself. I hoped with that last effort I would not find they were standing nearby waiting for me to make a gesture such as this.

All was eerily quiet as if the entire woods were holding its breath as well. From the ditch I crept slowly, measuring each step. I was barefooted now having run out of my boots and my socks. By the time I worked my way slowly and quietly through the dense terrain, taking care not to trip on some bramble, the soles of my feet were raw.

It had taken quite a while to reach the gravel road and I was totally exhausted physically and emotionally. I sat in the middle of the road contemplating my next move and listening to the night noise of the woods come alive once again. I patted down my body to see if there was anything crawling on me. As I did so I realized I had the sense to place my flashlight inside my pants pocket, an act I did not recall doing, but was ever so thankful I did. I decided I would wait for daylight to come before leaving the woods. However, soon after having spent some time listening to rustling in the brush, which I reasoned to be that of small mammals, rodents or the like, I was, nonetheless, getting quite anxious about spending the remainder of the night in the dark of the road. I decided it was safe to turn on my light. Retrieving it from my pocket I said a little prayer that it would shine for me and luckily…it did!

I could see instantly that my eight-legged friends had been busy as usual and had spun their labyrinth of webbing across the road for me, *thankyouverymuch*! But by now I was absolutely fearless. I simply took my time weaving and dodging my way between them and around them until I finally broke out into the coming of a new day. Hallelujah! It was already light but the sun was not up yet. I stood in the middle of Saloon Road looking back at the dense woods from which I had finally emerged.

The pavement under me feet was still cool and the rough texture of asphalt felt good to my bruised and aching feet. I had survived, not unscathed...but survived. God had let me live to at least see another day. Smiling in satisfaction, I turned to continue my journey home. Just then, off in the distance, I heard what sounded like a couple of whoops. That was all the encouragement I needed. C'mon, Mantan, I mused, jogging my weary body on bloodied feet the rest of the way down Saloon road until reaching the Poplar camp turn-off. Crossing over the cattle guard that stretched over the entrance I limped the short distance to the camp house. I wondered how the rest of the team had endured the evening. Nearing the camp-house I saw a couple of pickup trucks and a Sheriff Deputy's car parked on the front lawn. Upon opening the camp door you could've heard a pin-drop as a room full of astonished looking faces gawked at my entrance. I just stared back at them for a moment and then said, "WHAT?!"

That night after an exhausting day filled with interviews with the authorities, and news crews, and the debriefing with my team mates I finally arrived back home. After getting really clean in an hour long shower, and enjoying a hot meal, I crawled into my own bed. Oh, it felt heavenly lying on those cool sheets. The air was set to a perfect temperature and the hum of the compressor was a soothing sound in my ears. I stretched my weary, aching body long and hard before relaxing. I wanted to sleep so badly, but I was still wired from the experience and its follow-up. I wondered what kind of stir the events might create the next day.

My thoughts darted about like a house fly and I decided to reflect on the object in the sky rather than the monsters since the fireball was less odious I pondered briefly about the Martians. If they had landed there was gonna be hell to pay for someone... whoever that idiot navigator was that charted their course to land in the vast marshes of south Louisiana. "I pity da' fool!" I calculated at their speed the fireball could've been buried under many deposits of muck and mire. By the time the Martians finally dig out, they'll have to contend with gators and marsh mosquitoes. Oh, yeah... the marsh skeeters... there won't be a drop of...? Hmm, I queried. What if Martians don't have blood? No matter. We didn't have to worry much over their failed invasion.

Besides, even if they were lucky enough to overcome the odds of gators and skeeters, they'd still have to contend with the Cajun population who wouldn't take lightly to the disruption of their beloved marshes by a horde of ugly little aliens and who would, in all likelihood, take great pride in harvesting as many Martians as they possibly could. Certainly there would be no need of state issued tags, and just as certain, everyone would want a Martian mount to hang in their den. Yep! It was gonna be a rude awakening for the Martians and any other cosmic invaders... I envisioned the little green guys fighting off hordes of swamp people as wave upon wave of pissed-off Cajuns in airboats, armed to the teeth rained death and destruction upon them. Don't leave your death rays behind boys, you're gonna need 'em.

It had been an exhausting weekend to say the very least. Yet there would be no dreams of huge spiders, or of a Martian invasion, or of monstrous monsters lurking in the deep woods that would threaten my slumber. I smiled contentedly... closed my eyes and slept like a baby.

I am a long way from that awful night in the woods so many years ago. True to my vow, I haven't been in the woods since that night. I'm certain each of us in our own way holds onto some recollection of the phenomenon that occurred in the sky and in the woods that dark summer night. It was not a night forgotten easily and, we all have had to deal with it on our own terms. I still have nightmares, but not as often. The creatures we saw that night are still out there...somewhere, of that I am certain. I sometimes wonder... if they ever think of me...the one that stumbled yet managed to flee? I wonder...?

Fini

Printed in Great Britain
by Amazon

41853569R00030